Finn MacCool
and the
Giant's Causeway

by Malachy Doyle and Peter Utton

FRANKLIN WATTS
LONDON•SYDNEY

First published in 2009 by
Franklin Watts
338 Euston Road
London
NW1 3BH

Franklin Watts Australia
Level 17/207 Kent Street
Sydney
NSW 2000

Text © Malachy Doyle 2009
Illustrations © Peter Utton 2009

A CIP catalogue record for this book is available
from the British Library.

ISBN 978 0 7496 8550 8 (hbk)
ISBN 978 0 7496 8562 1 (pbk)

Series Editor: Jackie Hamley
Series Advisor: Dr Barrie Wade
Series Designer: Peter Scoulding

Printed in China

To find out more about Malachy Doyle
and his books, please visit:
www.malachydoyle.co.uk

Franklin Watts is a division of
Hachette Children's Books,
an Hachette UK company
www.hachette.co.uk

"I'm the strongest giant
in the whole wide world!"
roared Finn MacCool,
the mighty Irishman.

He was so loud that his voice travelled all the way to Scotland. "No, you're not!" boomed Benandonner, from the other side of the sea. "I'm stronger than you!"

Benandonner lobbed a gigantic rock over towards Ireland. Finn threw one back towards Scotland.

Soon there were the beginnings of a path, like a causeway, across the sea.

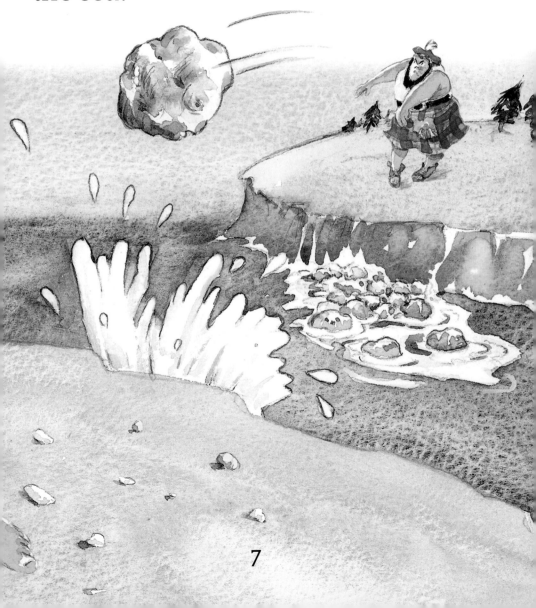

Then Una, Finn's wife, stopped him.
"He's twice your size, Finn!" she
warned him. "He'll eat you for
breakfast!"

8

"Is he?" said the Irish giant.
"What shall I do? With this new
causeway, he'll be over here by
morning."

"Here, put these on," said Una.
She dressed Finn in a nightie
and a frilly cap, and tucked
him into a gigantic cradle.

Then Una baked two massive cakes. In one of them, she hid a rod of iron.

Next morning, at daybreak,
the mighty Benandonner crossed
the rocky path from Scotland.
"Where's Finn MacCool?"
he boomed.

"He's in Scotland sorting out that
big bully, Benandonner," said Una.
"I'm Benandonner!" roared the
giant. "I'm here to sort HIM out!"
"Wait till he's back, then," said Una.
"He won't be long."

"While you're here, you can
help me," said Una.
"The wind's rattling the door.
Would you turn the house
round, like Finn does each day?"

14

Benandonner huffed and he
puffed, he puffed and he huffed.
He picked up the house in his two
massive arms and just about
managed to turn it round.

15

"Finn must be strong if he does
that every morning!" gasped
Benandonner.

"He is, indeed," said Una. "Here,
have one of his cakes." She gave
Benandonner the one with iron in.

"ARRGH!" yelled Benandonner,
spitting broken teeth.
"Finn likes them crunchy,"
said Una, hiding a smile.
"But stop your yelling, man.
You'll wake the baby!"

Just then, there was a mighty roar from the cradle. "WAAAA!"

"Good grief!" said Benandonner.

"How big is Finn, if that's his baby?"

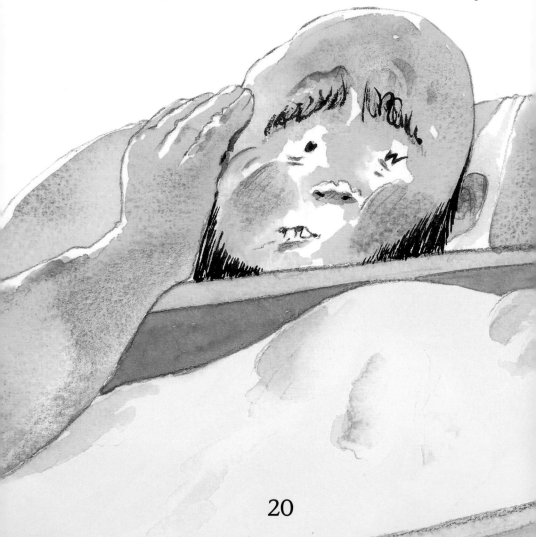

"Big," said Una. "Bigger than you!"
She reached in and gave the child
the second cake – the one without
iron in.

The baby munched.

The baby crunched.

The baby munched and crunched,
and burped.

"More!" he cried. "More! MORE!"

"He has a fine set of teeth on him," said Una, proudly.
"Put your finger in and feel them, Benandonner. Or are you scared?"

"Me? Scared?" said the Scottish giant. "I'm scared of nothing."

He put his hand in the baby's mouth. And Finn bit his middle finger clean off!

"My strength!" cried Benandonner.
"That's where I keep my strength!"

Before Una's eyes, he shrank, until he was only the size of a rabbit.

"Tell Finn I'll not be bothering him again," he peeped.

Then he was off, over the Giant's Causeway, and he never set foot in Ireland again.

Puzzle 1

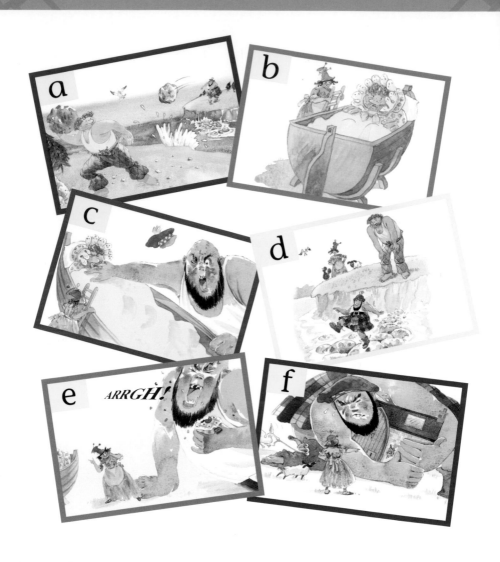

Put these pictures in the correct order.
Which event do you think is most important?
Now try writing the story in your own words!

Puzzle 2

Choose the correct speech bubbles for each character. Can you think of any others? Turn over to find the answers.

Answers

Puzzle 1

The correct order is: 1a, 2b, 3f, 4e, 5c, 6d

Puzzle 2

Finn MacCool: 4, 5

Benandonner: 1, 6

Una: 2, 3

Look out for more Hopscotch Adventures:

For more Hopscotch books go to:
www.franklinwatts.co.uk

* hardback   **Tales of Sinbad the Sailor also available!**